This Little Princess

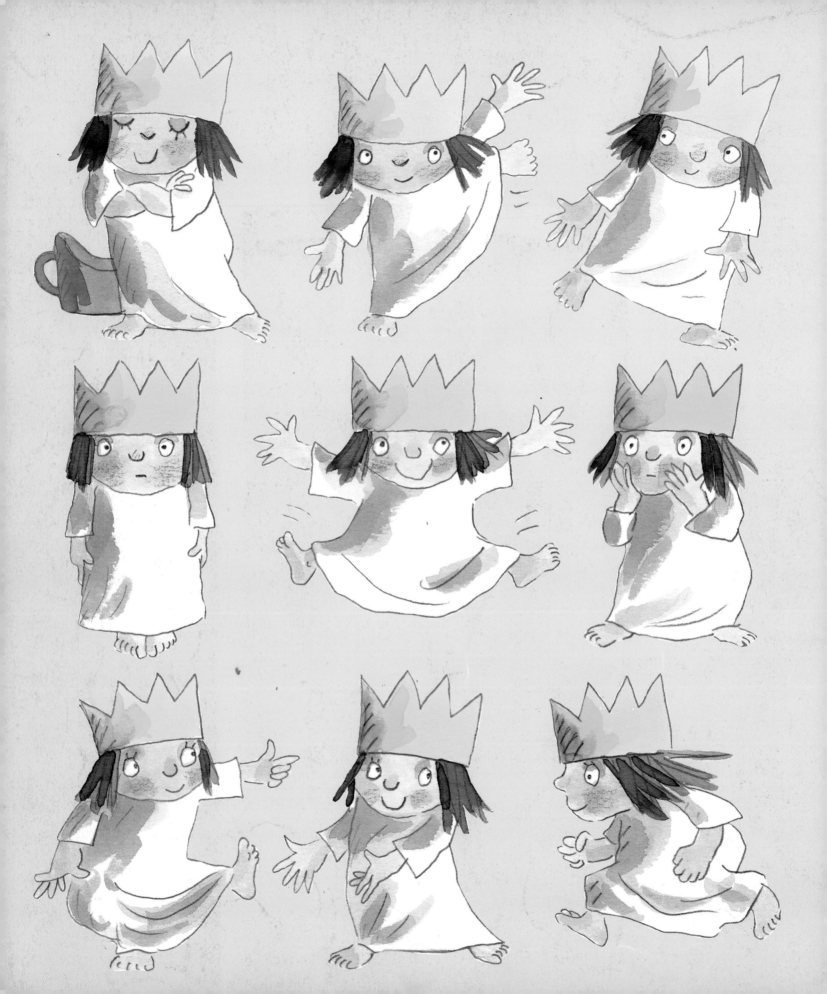

This paperback edition first published in 2013 by Andersen Press Ltd.
First published in Great Britain in 1993 by Andersen Press Ltd.,
20 Vauxhall Bridge Road, London SW1V 2SA.
Published in Australia by Random House Australia Pty.,
Level 3, 100 Pacific Highway, North Sydney, NSW 2060.
Text and illustration copyright © Tony Ross, 1993
The rights of Tony Ross to be identified as the author and illustrator
of this work have been asserted by him in accordance with
the Copyright, Designs and Patents Act, 1988.
All rights reserved.
Colour separated in Switzerland by Photolitho AG, Zürich.
Printed and bound in Singapore by Tien Wah Press.
Tony Ross has used pen, ink and watercolour in this book.

10   9   8   7   6   5   4   3   2   1

British Library Cataloguing in Publication Data available.

ISBN 978 1 84939 517 5

This book was printed on acid-free paper

A Little Princess Story

I Want to Be!

Tony Ross

Andersen Press

"The time has come to grow up," thought the Little Princess.

"I wonder how I should do it? Perhaps I should be different."

"But what sort of different should I be?"

"That's not what I should be. I'd better ask Mum."

"What is the best way to be?" she asked.
"Be kind . . ." said her mother,

". . . like your father."

"What is the best way to be?" the Little Princess asked.
"Be loving," said her father,

" . . . like your mother."

"What is the best way to be?" the Little Princess asked.
"Be clean," said the Cook.

"There is such a lot to remember," thought the Little Princess.
"I must be kind, loving and clean."

"What is the best way to be?" the Little Princess asked.
"Be brave," said the General.

"Be brave," thought the Little Princess.
"That's it! Then I could get spiders out of the bath myself."

"What is the best way to be?" the Little Princess asked.
"Be good at swimming . . ." said the Admiral,

" . . . then you will be safe if your boat ever sinks."

"What is the best way to be?" the Little Princess asked.
"Be clever," said the Prime Minister.

"And be healthy," said the Doctor.

"Oh dear!" thought the Little Princess. "I must be kind, loving and clean, brave, good at swimming, clever and healthy. I haven't got that many fingers!"

"Growing up is SO difficult."

"What is the best way to be?" asked the Little Princess.
"Oh, I don't know," said the Maid.

"I suppose the important question is . . . what do YOU want to be?"

"I want to be . . .

. . . TALL," said the Little Princess.

"But you ARE tall," said the Little Prince.

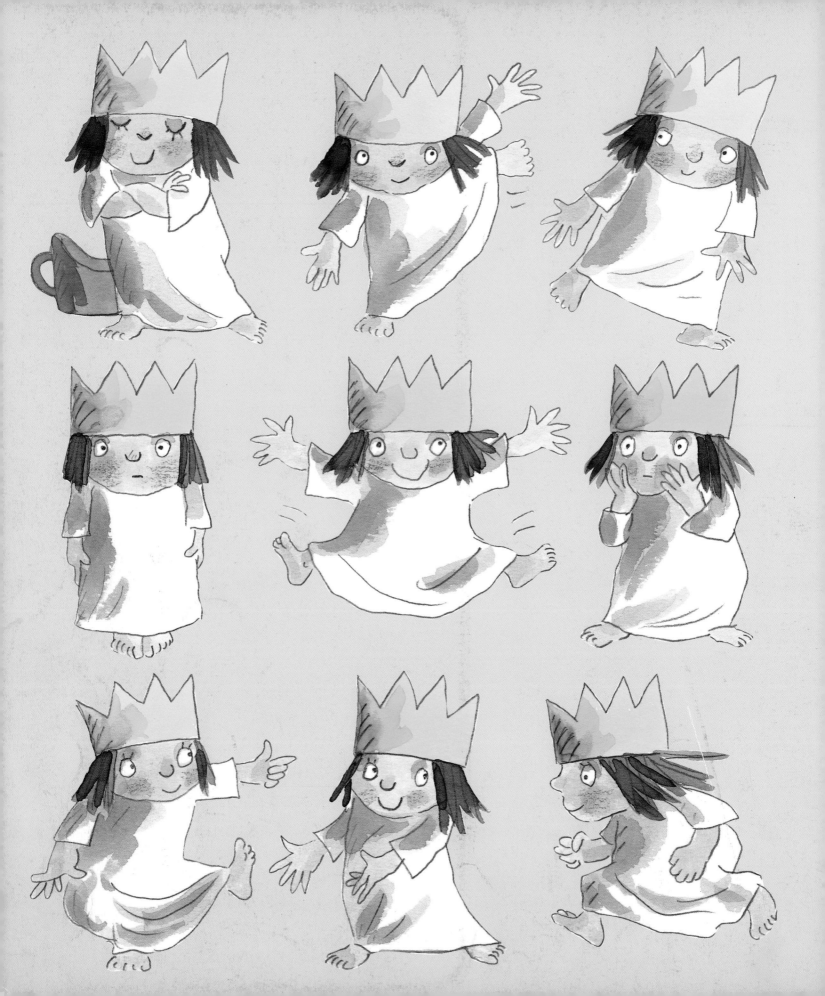

Other Little Princess Books

I Want My Potty!

I Want My Dinner!

I Want My Light On!

I Want My Present!

I Want a Sister!

I Want to Go Home!

I Want Two Birthdays!

I Want a Party!

I Want to Do it By Myself!

I Want to Win!

I Want My Dummy!

I Don't Want to Go to Hospital!

I Didn't Do it!

Little Princess titles are also available as eBooks.

LITTLE PRINCESS TV TIE-INS

Fun in the Sun!

I Want to Do Magic!

I Want My Sledge!

I Don't Like Salad!

I Don't Want to Comb My Hair!

I Want to Go to the Fair!

I Want to Be a Cavegirl!

I Want to Be Tall!

I Want My Sledge! Book and DVD